GOOD MORNING AMIRA

WRITTEN BY MELICA NICCOLE
AND AMIRA AYOBAMI

ILLUSTRATED BY
VIVIANA MOYANO

PUBLISHED IN 2021
BY MELICA NICCOLE
AND HAMPTON PUBLISHING HOUSE, LLC

Learn with Amira

 Teddy Bear

 Soap

 Dog

 Hair Brush

 Toothbrush

 Duck

Good Morning Amira

Paper doll game.
Ask a grown up to help you cut the pieces and have fun!

Count the Ducks

How many ducks do you see?

Count the Dogs
How many dogs do you see?

Thank you for reading our book.

Look out for other titles
by Amira Ayobami
and Melica Niccole soon.

Both can be found on
Instagram
under their author names.

Printed in Great Britain
by Amazon